A FLOWER FAIRIES
BRACELET BOOK
CICELY MARY BARKER
FREDERICK WARNE

*The reproductions in this book have been made using the most modern electronic
scanning methods from entirely new transparencies of Cicely Mary Barker's
original watercolours. They enable Cicely Mary Barker's skill as an artist
to be appreciated as never before*

FREDERICK WARNE
Published by the Penguin Group
Penguin Books Ltd, 27 Wrights Lane, London W8 5TZ, England
Penguin Books USA Inc., 375 Hudson Street, New York, N.Y. 10014, USA
Penguin Books Australia Ltd, Ringwood, Victoria, Australia
Penguin Books Canada Ltd, 10 Alcorn Avenue, Toronto, Ontario, Canada M4V 3B2
Penguin Books (N.Z.) Ltd, 182-190 Wairau Road, Auckland 10, New Zealand

Penguin Books Ltd, Registered Offices: Harmondsworth, Middlesex, England

First published 1996
1 3 5 7 9 10 8 6 4 2

ISBN 0 7232 4293 3

Colour reproduction by Saxon Photolitho Ltd, Norwich
Printed in China by Imago Publishing Ltd

◆ MY PAGE ◆

This Flower Fairies book belongs to

. . . .

My birthday is on . . . .

I am . . . . . . years and . . . . . . months old

My address is . . . .

. . . .

. . . .

My school is . . . .

My best friend's name is . . . .

My favourite colour is . . . .

My favourite Flower Fairy is

. . . .

◆ THE SONG OF ◆
THE ALMOND BLOSSOM FAIRY

Joy! the Winter's nearly gone!
Soon will Spring come dancing on;
And, before her, here dance I,
Pink like sunrise in the sky.
Other lovely things will follow;
Soon will cuckoo come, and swallow;
Birds will sing and buds will burst,
But the Almond is the first!

The Almond Blossom Fairy

The Forget-me-not Fairy

◆ THE SONG OF ◆
THE FORGET-ME-NOT FAIRY

Where do fairy babies lie
Till they're old enough to fly?
Here's a likely place, I think,
'Mid these flowers, blue and pink,
(Pink for girls and blue for boys:
Pretty things for babies' toys!)
Let us peep now, gently. Why,
Fairy baby, here you lie!

Kicking there, with no one by,
Baby dear, how good you lie!
All alone, but O, you're not—
You could *never* be—forgot!
O how glad I am I've found you,
With Forget-me-nots around you,
Blue, the colour of the sky!
Fairy baby, Hushaby!

◆ THE SONG OF ◆
THE BEECH TREE FAIRY

The trunks of Beeches are smooth and grey,
  Like tall straight pillars of stone
In great Cathedrals where people pray;
  Yet from tiny things they've grown.
About their roots is the moss; and wide
  Their branches spread, and high;
It seems to us, on the earth who bide,
  That their heads are in the sky.

And when Spring is here,
  and their leaves appear,
    With a silky fringe on each,
Nothing is seen so new and green
  As the new young green of Beech.
O the great grey Beech is young, is young,
  When, dangling soft and small,
Round balls of bloom from its twigs are hung,
  And the sun shines over all.

The Beech Tree Fairy

The Lilac Fairy

◆ THE SONG OF ◆
THE LILAC FAIRY

White May is flowering,
   Red May beside;
Laburnum is showering
   Gold far and wide;
But *I* sing of Lilac,
   The dearly-loved Lilac,
Lilac, in Maytime
   A joy and a pride!

I love her so much
   That I never can tell
If she's sweeter to look at,
   Or sweeter to smell.

◆ THE SONG OF ◆
THE GERANIUM FAIRY

Red, red, vermilion red,
With buds and blooms in a glorious head!
There isn't a flower, the wide world through,
That glows with a brighter scarlet hue.
Her name—Geranium—ev'ryone knows;
She's just as happy wherever she grows,
In an earthen pot or a garden bed—
Red, red, vermilion red!

The Geranium Fairy

The Sweet Pea Fairies

◆ THE SONG OF ◆
THE SWEET PEA FAIRIES

Here Sweet Peas are climbing;
  (Here's the Sweet Pea rhyme!)
Here are little tendrils,
  Helping them to climb.

Here are sweetest colours;
  Fragrance very sweet;
Here are silky pods of peas,
  Not for us to eat!

Here's a fairy sister,
  Trying on with care
Such a grand new bonnet
  For the baby there.

Does it suit you, Baby?
  Yes, I really think
Nothing's more becoming
  Than this pretty pink!

◆ THE SONG OF ◆
THE WHITE BINDWEED FAIRY

O long long stems that twine!
O buds, so neatly furled!
O great white bells of mine,
(None purer in the world)
Each lasting but one day!
O leafy garlands, hung
In wreaths beside the way—
Well may your praise be sung!

(But this Bindweed, which is a big sister to the little pink
Field Convolvulus, is not good to have in gardens, though it is
so beautiful; because it winds around other plants and trees.
One of its names is "Hedge Strangler". Morning Glories are
a garden kind of Convolvulus.)

The White Bindweed Fairy

The Michaelmas Daisy Fairy

◆ THE SONG OF ◆
THE MICHAELMAS DAISY FAIRY

"Red Admiral, Red Admiral,
   I'm glad to see you here,
      Alighting on my daisies one by one!
I hope you like their flavour
   and although the Autumn's near,
      Are happy as you sit there in the sun?"

"I thank you very kindly, sir!
   Your daisies *are* so nice,
      So pretty and so plentiful are they;
The flavour of their honey, sir,
   it really does entice;
      I'd like to bring my brothers, if I may!"

"Friend butterfly, friend butterfly,
   go fetch them one and all!
      I'm waiting here to welcome every guest;
And tell them it is Michaelmas,
   and soon the leaves will fall,
      But *I* think Autumn sunshine is the best!"

◆ THE SONG OF ◆
THE BLACKBERRY FAIRY

My berries cluster black and thick
For rich and poor alike to pick.

I'll tear your dress, and cling, and tease,
And scratch your hands and arms and knees.

I'll stain your fingers and your face,
And then I'll laugh at your disgrace.

But when the bramble-jelly's made,
You'll find your trouble well repaid.

The Blackberry Fairy

The Wayfaring Tree Fairy

◆ THE SONG OF ◆
THE WAYFARING TREE FAIRY

My shoots are tipped with buds as dusty-grey
As ancient pilgrims toiling on their way.

Like Thursday's child with far to go, I stand,
All ready for the road to Fairyland;

With hood, and bag, and shoes, my name to suit,
And in my hand my gorgeous-tinted fruit.

◆ THE SONG OF ◆
THE OLD MAN'S BEARD FAIRY

This is where the little elves
Cuddle down to hide themselves;
Into fluffy beds they creep,
Say good-night, and go to sleep.

(Old-Man's Beard is Wild Clematis; its flowers are called
Traveller's Joy. This silky fluff belongs to the seeds.)

The Old Man's Beard Fairy

The Winter Jasmine Fairy

◆ THE SONG OF ◆
THE WINTER JASMINE FAIRY

All through the Summer my leaves were green,
But never a flower of mine was seen;
Now Summer is gone, that was so gay,
And my little green leaves are shed away.
       In the grey of the year
       What cheer, what cheer?

The Winter is come, the cold winds blow;
I shall feel the frost and the drifting snow;
But the sun can shine in December too,
And this is the time of my gift to you.
       See here, see here,
       My flowers appear!

The swallows have flown beyond the sea,
But friendly Robin, he stays with me;
And little Tom-Tit, so busy and small,
Hops where the jasmine is thick on the wall;
       And we say: "Good cheer!
       We're here! We're here!"

PLANTAIN AND MOON-DAISY DANCING TOGETHER,
ALL THROUGH THE BEAUTIFUL SUNSHINY WEATHER.